K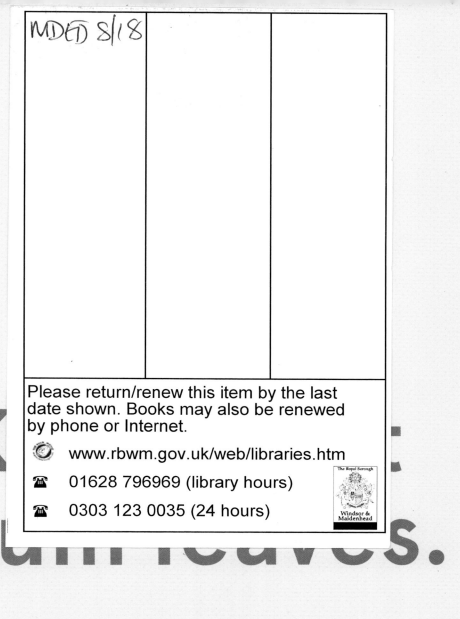
gum leaves.

LAURA + PHILIP BUNTING

This is a koala.

Koalas eat gum leaves.
Nothing but gum leaves.
All day. Every day.
So many gum leaves.

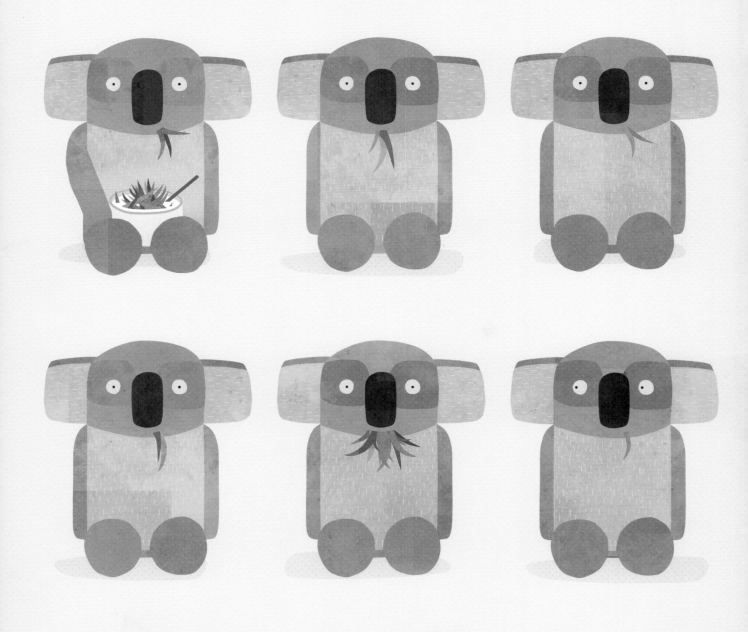

Gum leaves for breakfast.
Gum leaves for lunch.
Gum leaves for dinner.
With no exceptions...

Not even on their birthday.

Most koalas don't seem to mind.

But this one
does.

This koala has had enough.
He won't eat another leaf.
Not another gumdrop.

He's on the lookout for
some tastier tucker.

No.

No!

Woah.

Hello!

Whoosh!

#%*@!*

*By gum, that's good!

He runs.

He jumps.

He dances.

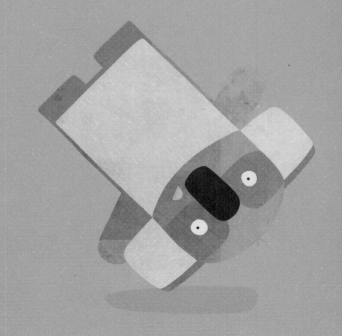

He cartwheels.

He goes back
for more.

Now this koala eats ice-cream.
Nothing but ice-cream.
All day. Every day.
So many ice-creams.

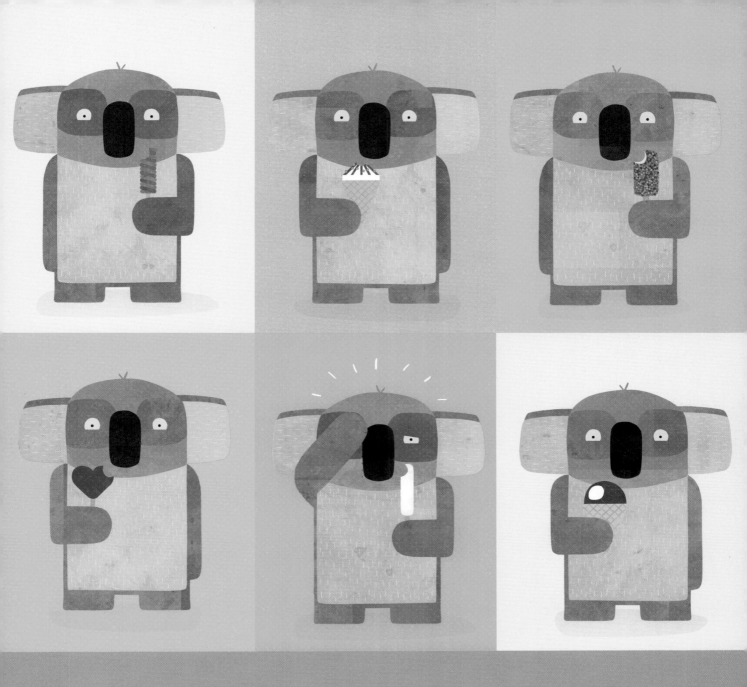

Ice-cream for breakfast.
Ice-cream for lunch.
Ice-cream for dinner.
With no exceptions . . .

Until one day, he had enough.
He couldn't eat another cone.
Not one more scoop.

It was time to go home.

#@$%!*

*By gum, this is hard work.

Koalas don't eat ice-cream.

Koalas eat gum leaves.

Even this one.

Most of the time.

FOR LEO,
WITH LOVE XX

**Despite their monotonous diet, koalas are very fussy eaters.
There are around 700 varieties of gum leaf to choose from in
Australia, but koalas usually stick to just a few select species.**

First published in 2017 by Omnibus Books
An imprint of Scholastic Australia Pty Limited

First published in the UK in 2018 by Scholastic Children's Books
Euston House, 24 Eversholt Street
London NW1 1DB
A division of Scholastic Ltd
www.scholastic.co.uk
London ~ New York ~ Toronto ~ Sydney ~ Auckland
Mexico City ~ New Delhi ~ Hong Kong

Text copyright © Laura Bunting 2017
Illustrations copyright © Philip Bunting 2017

ISBN 978 1407 18870 6